WE LOVE THIS BOOK:

It's Monstrously funny!

It introduces the naughtiest (but nicest) teacher you'll ever meet!

It's packed full of brilliant characters that you'll love.

Illustrations pop off the page like fireworks.

...ntains ...ts!

'Oh, sorry. I forgot Granny was staying over,' Jake mumbled.

'Actually, she was supposed to be coming next week but she got her dates mixed up and—'

BRIIIIIIIIIIIIIIIIING! The phone rang.

'For heaven's sake . . .' Mum went to answer it. Out of the corner of his eye, Jake spotted a small furry lightning bolt shoot past the kitchen door. Two seconds later, Connie waddled past at top speed, crying.

'SILLY DOGGY! WON'T PUT NAPPY ON!'

Jake nearly dropped his Fruitloops.

'Yes Alan, the paperwork's ready . . .' Mum was saying. Jake edged out of the kitchen and ran down the hall. *Where'd creature go?* He heard a voice from the living room.

'Is that you, Jakey? Where's my kiss?'

Granny!

He screeched to a halt outside the door.

'Have you grown a beard, dear? Goodness, children grow up fast nowadays!'

Puzzled, Jake pushed the door open.

Creature was squatting on Granny's lap, puckering up his lips . . .

This book is dedicated to my son Owen, a small,
cheeky creature who eats mainly biscuits—S.W.

To Sarah McIntyre—D.O'C.

OXFORD
UNIVERSITY PRESS

Great Clarendon Street, Oxford OX2 6DP

Oxford University Press is a department of the University of Oxford.
It furthers the University's objective of excellence in research, scholarship,
and education by publishing worldwide. Oxford is a registered trade mark of
Oxford University Press in the UK and in certain other countries

Text copyright © Sam Watkins 2015
Illustrations copyright © David O'Connell 2015

The moral rights of the author and artist have been asserted

Database right Oxford University Press (maker)

First published 2015

British Library Cataloguing in Publication Data available

Data available

ISBN: 978-0-19-274265-0 (paperback)
ISBN: 978-0-19-274266-7 (eBook)

2 4 6 8 10 9 7 5 3 1

Printed in Great Britain

Paper used in the production of this book is a natural,
recyclable product made from wood grown in sustainable forests.
The manufacturing process conforms to the environmental
regulations of the country of origin

CREATURE TEACHER

SAM WATKINS and
ILLUSTRATED BY David O'Connell

OXFORD
UNIVERSITY PRESS

RULE 1:

DO NOT GROAN LOUDLY WHEN
ASKED TO RECITE POETRY

B-R-R-R-R-R-R-R-R-R-R-R-R-R-R-
RINNNNNGGGGGGGGGGGGGG-G-G-G!

The school bell screeched in Jake's ear and
he leapt out of the chair with a yelp.

It's a new school, not a shark tank, he told
himself, sitting once more. *But then again—
what if his teacher was an old dragon? What if
he didn't make any friends? What if . . .*

1

The office door burst open and the secretary bustled out. 'I'll take you to the Head now, dear . . . oops, mind yourself . . . '

Jake found himself being propelled through a stream of noisy pupils that had erupted from nowhere. Minutes later, the corridor was empty again. The secretary stopped outside a door.

On it was a sign that read '**MRS BLUNT**' in large, angry letters. Underneath, in smaller, slightly annoyed letters, it said 'Headteacher'.

'Wait here,' said the secretary. 'The Head will be out shortly.'

A well-disciplined row of chairs stood along the wall and Jake perched on one. A man sat at the other end, his knees nearly grazing his ears. He wore black-rimmed glasses and was tapping a rhythm on his knee.

'MUPPETS!' he exclaimed suddenly.

Jake jumped.

The man chuckled. 'Sorry. I've been trying to work out what that rhythm was and it just struck me—it's the theme from *The Muppet Show*.' He looked at Jake over his glasses.

'Seeing the Head? Are you in trouble?'

'No. It's my first day,' said Jake.

'Ah. I'm a new boy too. Name's Hyde. And you are . . . ?'

'Jake Jones.'

'Delighted to meet you, Jake Jones. Are you nervous?'

Jake lied. 'No.'

'Me neither,' said Mr Hyde. He looked flushed. 'How scary can the Head be, anyway? She won't bite, will she? Heh heh.'

Mr Hyde had gone very red indeed. Even his ears were scarlet. *And—was he actually starting to . . . glow?* Jake wondered.

'If I was nervous,' continued Mr Hyde, 'I'd just tap a rhythm on my knee. Like this.' Mr Hyde drummed his fingers up and down gently on his leg.

Tap-tap-tappity-tap.

Jake rubbed his eyes and looked at Mr Hyde

again. He was a bit pink, but he wasn't glowing.

Suddenly the Headteacher's door burst open and Mr Hyde started tapping his knee furiously.

'MR HYDE! COME IN!' a harsh voice commanded.

Mr Hyde took a deep breath, stood up, and ducked in through the door. It clanged shut.

Jake stared at the closed door. *Had Mr Hyde actually glowed*? He shook his head. He must have imagined it . . . *People don't glow.*

Before Jake had time to think about this, the door opened again. Mr Hyde shuffled out, followed by a dark-haired woman in a suit. She saw Jake, and frowned.

'Oh yes. The new boy. This is your teacher, Mr Hyde. Now, let's get you both to class.'

Mrs Blunt marched them out into a courtyard

with a huge pile of rocks in the middle. She stopped by the rocks, and patted one of them fondly.

'This is my Rockery. All the building work is done by pupils who earn three Sad Faces. A Sad Face is given for breaking one of the School Rules.'

Jake's eyes met Mr Hyde's. The rocks looked very heavy.

'Our discipline is first-rate,' Mrs Blunt continued, leading them into a corridor, her heels click-clacking on the hard

floor. 'I hope you will keep 5b in order, Mr Hyde. They can be . . . lively.'

Jake heard the sound of chatter, getting louder and louder. As they rounded a corner, he saw a gaggle of pupils outside a classroom door. There was pushing, shoving, and loud giggling.

'*Mrs Blunt!*' one of the girls hissed.

The children scurried into line. The hubbub faded. One boy dropped his lunchbox and biscuits rolled across the corridor. He bent to pick them up.

'McCRUMB!' roared Mrs Blunt.

The boy groaned. 'Miiiiss . . . ' but got back in line.

'Class 5b. Anyone wishing to work on the Rockery, continue talking. If not, go in, sit down and do not utter a sound.'

The class trooped in. Mrs Blunt stopped the biscuit dropper.

'Barnaby McCrumb. I believe you have two Sad Faces. One more, and I will see you at the Rockery. Understand?'

'Yeeeessss, miss.'

Mrs Blunt glared at Barnaby, but waved him into the silent classroom and marched Jake and Mr Hyde to the front.

'5b, meet Jake Jones, your new classmate,' said Mrs Blunt.

Twenty-five pairs of eyes fixed on Jake. He would rather have been dangling upside down over a tank full of sharks.

'And this is your new teacher, Mr Hyde. To welcome them, I want you to recite my 'Joy of School Rules' poem you've been working on for the Founders' Celebration.'

There was a chorus of groans.

'QUIET! I did *not* give you permission to groan.'

A girl in the front row put her hand up.

'Nora?'

'Miss, we haven't practised for *a-a-a-ages*

because Miss Read said it brought her out in a rash but I thought it might be a tarantula bite because tarantula hairs contain a deadly toxin—'

A boy behind Nora broke in.

'I wrote a tune for it, Miss. Shall I sing it for you?'

'I'm not interested in songs about tarantula hair, Karl. I'm interested in Class 5b reciting my poem at the Founders' Celebration tomorrow: word perfect, with gusto.'

She turned to Mr Hyde.

'The Founders' Evening is an extremely important event, at which all the classes put on a performance to show their appreciation of the people who established our wonderful school and its *excellent* Rules.'

She pointed to a large poster on the back

wall of the classroom. At the top was written 'THE SCHOOL RULES'. At the bottom of the poster was a photo of the Head herself, glaring furiously out at anyone unlucky enough to be looking.

'The four remaining Founders will be attending, and parents and local press are invited. Unfortunately, Class 5b are a *long* way behind in their rehearsals.'

Her eyes bored into those of Mr Hyde. 'But under your direction, Mr Hyde, I'm sure they will come along in leaps and bounds.'

Jake saw Mr Hyde smile uneasily as Mrs Blunt turned smartly on her heels and clicked menacingly out of the classroom.

RULE 2:

NEVER
∧ KNOW EXACTLY HOW
MANY SCHOOL RULES
THERE ARE

CLICK-CLICK-CLICK-CLICK... BANG!

The door slammed behind Mrs Blunt so hard that several books leapt off the shelf in fright. Jake and Mr Hyde jumped too.

Mr Hyde caught Jake's eye and winked.

'First things first,' he said. 'Jake, you need somewhere to sit.' He looked round. 'Park yourself next to the young arachnologist in the front row. Nora, isn't it?'

'Yes, sir.' She looked pleased.

Jake sat down next to Nora. She squinted at him through her glasses.

'Do you want to see my slug collection?' she asked. 'I've got about two hundred . . .'

'Um—' Jake began but he was saved from answering as Mr Hyde went on.

'Secondly. This poem. I'm sure you're much better than you think. In fact I'll eat my hat if you're not utterly brilliant!'

'I wouldn't, sir,' said a boy with a droopy fringe that covered half his face. 'We are pretty bad. And the poem is s-o-o-ooo boring . . .'

14

Mr Hyde clearly wasn't prepared to believe bad of anyone or anything. He bounded around, moving desks.

'Okay—everyone on the floor!' Mr Hyde lay down.

Is he crazy? Jake looked round. There were a few sniggers.

'Action stations, 5b! Lying down, breathing deeply!'

Slowly, the class did as they were told. There wasn't much deep breathing, although Jake could hear a lot of high-pitched giggling.

After a minute of this, Mr Hyde jumped to his feet and stood, wobbling, on one leg, arms in the air. The class stood up and did the same.

Mr Hyde did a massive wobble and he fell over.

'Sir, do you want *us* to do that?' asked Nora, puzzled.

He got up, straightening his glasses.

'Um, no, that's enough yoga for today,' he said. 'Let's hear this poem. Jake, come and be an extra pair of ears.'

Jake and Mr Hyde perched on a desk while everyone else lined up at the front. Mr Hyde did a drum roll with his hands.

'Class 5b present . . . "THE JOY OF SCHOOL RULES"!' he announced.

There was nervous shuffling. Then Karl stepped forward and began:

'The School Rules make us happy,
Every girl and every boy.
We're grateful to our Glorious Head
For bringing us such joy.'

Karl stepped back into line.

Jake squirmed. Karl did not look in the least bit joyful. Nor did anyone else. Mr Hyde's smile faded slightly, but he nodded encouragingly. After some confused whispering, a girl wearing football kit was shoved forward. She looked at Karl.

'How does my verse start?'

'The School Rules are incredible . . .'

'Oh yeah.' She took a deep breath:

The School Rules are incredible—
All one hundred and *forty-two* . . . '

Nora broke in. 'One hundred and forty-one, Alexis! Look at the poster.'

Jake looked at the School Rules poster properly for the first time. *A hundred and forty-one school rules!* He gulped. His old school had only ten! Mrs Blunt's photo was glaring at him as if he'd broken at least half of them.

'Okay, okay ... one hundred and forty-one ...' Alexis continued.

'Hang on—the poem says a hundred and forty-two,' said Karl.

Nora glared at him. 'What's Rule 142, then?'

'Maybe it's new,' suggested Alexis.

'Okay, what is this new rule, then?' Nora crossed her arms defiantly.

Karl laughed. 'Rule 142 is . . . Slugs are not permitted in the classroom.'

Nora frowned. 'Leave my slugs out of this! They don't do any harm—'

'One of them slimed me yesterday,' said someone.

'One scoffed my salad!' called someone else. The class fell about laughing.

'Calm down, everyone,' called Mr Hyde.

No one calmed down.

'Stop hassling Nora, guys,' said the boy with the fringe.

'Woodstock, you're only saying that because she helps you with your science homework!' someone called.

The whole class was bickering. Jake glanced around to see if Mr Hyde was going to do something, but he had disappeared. Then—

'A-WOP-BOP-A-LOO-BOP-A-LOP-BAM-BOOM!'

The class froze. Loud music was belting out from speakers at the front of the classroom. Mr Hyde popped up from behind a computer.

'Zumba time!' he bellowed above the music. 'Exercise will get the creative juices flowing!'

He started lurching around violently. Everyone stared, open-mouthed.

'What's he doing?' Jake heard a voice whisper nearby. Nora had slid back into her seat and was gaping at Mr Hyde.

'Dancing, I think,' he whispered back.

'5B, GET READY TO BOOGIE!' shouted Mr Hyde. 'Whatever I do, you follow. I'm warning you though, it's not easy to dance like me . . . '

A few pupils tittered. Jake suddenly realized—Mr Hyde was distracting the class from the argument. *Clever*!

Mr Hyde started to clap to the music. 'Join in, everyone!'

Jake nudged Nora. 'Come on.'

'I don't dance—'

'You do now.' Jake pulled her to her feet. He started to clap. After a moment, Nora joined in. Seconds later, Alexis and Karl followed.

Mr Hyde waggled his hands to the side. Woodstock and a few others did the same.

He shook his head. About twelve pupils shook their heads. Woodstock's fringe flapped madly. Nora's glasses fell off.

Mr Hyde did the Twist— everyone twisted madly! He did the Macarena, the Moonwalk, and the

Monkey, the class following his every move. Nora danced on a table! Woodstock did a headspin! Karl tossed Alexis in the air—which would have been more impressive if he'd caught her too.

A-WOP-BOP-A-LOO-BOP-A-LOP-BAM-BOOM!

Abruptly, the music ended.

Jake collapsed into a chair, panting. Everyone looked zonked except Mr Hyde.

'Well done, everyone! You are a groovy bunch . . . Yes, Barnaby?'

Barnaby smirked. 'Sir, you

said you'd eat your hat if we weren't very good at reading the poem.'

'And so I shall,' declared Mr Hyde, 'if we don't get a standing ovation at the Founders' Celebration tomorrow!'

At that moment, the bell rang. Mr Hyde clapped his hands.

'Lunchtime! Off you go, folks. Take your time. I've got things I need to prepare for this afternoon.'

'What are we doing this afternoon?' asked Woodstock.

Mr Hyde smiled mysteriously. 'Wait and see . . . '

RULE 3:

ALWAYS
~~NEVER~~ TELL AMELIA
TROTTER-HOGG
WHAT TO DO

Jake found himself swept along in a babbling torrent of pupils towards the canteen. He heard snippets of gossip from some of his class.

' . . . said he'd eat his hat!'

' . . . dances like my dad . . . '

Jake grinned. His new school was more interesting than he'd thought it would be!

There was a monster queue in the canteen.

Slowly, Jake shuffled forwards till he reached the front. He grabbed a plate of spaghetti, then looked around for a seat. Most tables seemed to be full. Then across the hall, he spotted Nora at a table on her own and wound his way through the chaos till he reached her. She had a plate of salad in front of her.

'Hi,' he said awkwardly. 'Um . . . can I sit here?'

She looked up.

'Of course. You don't mind sharing a table with Sylvester, do you?'

She pointed at her salad. A humungous orange slug was oozing happily away on a piece of lettuce. Jake hesitated, then shook his head and sat down.

'No. Why should I?'

He took a mouthful of lunch. 'Eurrrgh!' He put his fork down. 'Think I'll have the salad tomorrow,' he said, looking enviously at Sylvester.

Nora nodded wisely. 'Slugs know best.'

Just then, the boy with the long fringe appeared. He flopped in the chair next to Nora, and pushed his fringe to one side to look at Jake.

'Hey,' he said. 'Jake, isn't it?

'Yep,' said Jake. 'You're Woodstock, right?'

Woodstock nodded. He got a sketchbook out and started to scribble.

Jake leaned over to watch.

Woodstock's pen flew across the paper. A scribble became a person . . . glasses and a white shirt turned it into Mr Hyde . . . then with the addition of a quiff and sunglasses, Mr

Hyde became Elvis Presley.

Jake laughed. 'That's brilliant!'

'So what do we think of Mr Hyde?' Woodstock asked.

'I like him,' Nora said. 'He called me an arachnologist.'

'Yeah, he seems cool,' said Woodstock. 'Better than Mr Sharp, anyway.' He turned to Jake. 'He made us clean the toilets with our toothbrushes!'

Jake's eyes widened. 'Why did he do that?'

'He's Mrs Blunt's cousin,' said Nora.

'And Mrs Blunt,' explained Woodstock, 'is a

horrid old dragon.'

Jake laughed. 'Well, Mr Hyde seems re nice . . .'

He heard a snigger, and looked around. At the next table he saw a snooty-faced girl with a ponytail staring at them. She caught Jake's eye and pulled a face, then started whispering to two other girls. They turned and stared at Jake. 'Mr Hyde seems *REALLY* nice!' the girl with the ponytail mimicked in a silly voice. All the girls laughed.

Jake flushed and turned away.

'Who's that girl with the ponytail?' he asked Nora and Woodstock in a low voice.

Amelia Trotter-Hogg from Class 5a.' Nora frowned.

'The Most Annoying Person in the World,'

Woodstock added.

'Universe,' Nora corrected. 'She's Mrs Blunt's pet pupil.'

The bell rang. Jake stood up but Nora stopped him. 'That's the warning bell. We've got ten minutes yet.'

Woodstock was adding some finishing touches to his drawing.

'Finished,' he said, putting his pen down.

Jake craned over to see. 'Awesome. You should show it to Mr Hyde,' he said.

Woodstock grinned. 'I will! You know—I think we've finally got a really amazing teacher—'

SPLOOOOOSH!

'Ooops,' said a sugary voice. 'I accidentally spilt my juice all over your *amazing* new teacher.'

Jake and Nora jumped up, but poor Woodstock sat glued to his chair in shock. Juice streamed down his nose and dripped onto his drawing. Amelia Trotter-Hogg was standing behind him with an upturned cup in her hand.

'You—you—' Woodstock spluttered.

'You did that on purpose!' Nora cried.

'How would you know, goggle-girl?' Amelia hissed.

Jake's blood started to boil. 'Don't speak to Nora like that!'

'Shut up, new boy! New boys don't order me around. In fact, no one orders me arou . . . '

Amelia's voice slithered away. Jake glanced up to see Mrs Blunt striding into the canteen. In an instant, Amelia changed from viper to kitten.

'Mrs Blunt! Mrs Blunt, hellooooo!' She skipped across the hall towards the Headteacher.

Jake and Nora ran to get paper towels to dry

the dripping Woodstock off.

'My picture's ruined,' Woodstock groaned. Jake tried to cheer him up.

'It's not too bad. Actually, that splodge looks cool . . . '

'Move along, you lot. Goodness, what a mess!' A dinner lady shooed them away.

They walked back to class across the deserted playground. Well, almost deserted. Jake saw a boy crouching in a corner, sweet wrappers dancing around him in the breeze. It was Barnaby. Nora saw him too, and gasped in horror.

'Oh NO! Barnaby's eating sweets!' She started running towards him.

Jake looked puzzled. 'So . . . ?'

'Barnaby's not allowed sweets,' Woodstock

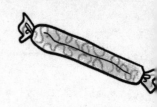

said. 'They send him loopy.'

They followed Nora.

'Barnaby, where did you get those sweets?'
Nora was asking.

'Nuuffink thoo dooo wiv yooo,' mumbled
Barnaby through a mouthful of chocolate.

'Someone gave them to you!' exclaimed Nora.
'Who was it?'

Barnaby shrugged, but his eyes slid across
the playground and rested on someone for just
a second too long.

Jake followed the line of Barnaby's gaze.
Amelia again! She was walking towards them,
her two sniggering friends in tow. She tossed
her hair.

'Hanging out with the geeks,
Barnaby?'

Barnaby scowled. 'I'm not hanging out with them.'

Nora rounded on Amelia. 'It was you! You gave Barnaby sweets, didn't you! Why did you do that?'

'I know,' said Woodstock angrily. 'So he'll make trouble for Mr Hyde!'

'Oh dear, do you think he will?' gasped Amelia in fake horror. 'Poor amazing Mr Hyde.'

The other girls giggled. Amelia turned to Barnaby. 'Remember what we talked about? Bet you're too scared . . .'

She walked away, laughing.

Jake turned to

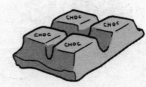

Barnaby. 'What did she mean? What're you too scared to do?'

Barnaby jumped up, wiping chocolate from his mouth.

'I'm not scared of anything—I'm Barnaby McCrumb! Teachers beware, the McCrumb Menace is on the warpath . . .'

He raced off, a crazed look in his eyes.

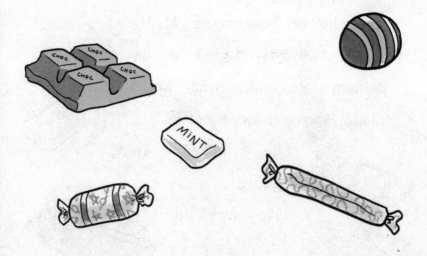

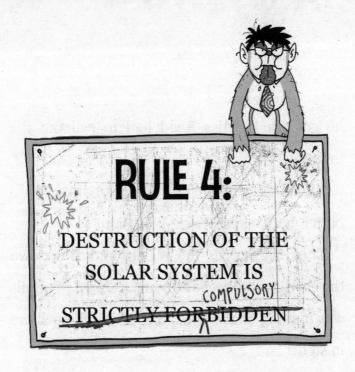

RULE 4:

DESTRUCTION OF THE SOLAR SYSTEM IS ~~STRICTLY FORBIDDEN~~ COMPULSORY

Nora groaned. 'He's going to be a nightmare.'

'Will he really be *that* bad?' asked Jake. 'It's just a few sweets.'

'Last time he ate sweets he rode a cleaning trolley round the school and crashed it in the pond,' said Nora grimly.

'The time before he climbed on the roof and made monkey noises,' said Woodstock. 'Then he got stuck. Miss Read had to call the fire brigade.'

'Okay—maybe you're right,' said Jake. 'We'd better get back to class quick, then!'

They ran across the playground and down the corridor to the classroom. A crowd of pupils was jostling at the door. Barnaby was nowhere in sight.

'What's happening?' Jake asked a girl. She pointed at a sign on the door.

'PREPARE FOR THE JOURNEY OF A LIFETIME!'

Journey? The talking petered out. Mr Hyde had appeared in the doorway.

'Class 5b, your spaceship awaits . . . '

Alexis was first in. Jake heard her gasp. 'Ooooooh . . . '

The next pupil went in. 'Aaaaaaah . . . '

Jake stepped through the door. It was dark, and his eyes took a moment to adjust. He looked up.

'Wow . . . '

Around the ceiling hung glowing globes, some greenish-blue, some fiery orange and red. One had rings. *The planets!* In the middle hung the largest and brightest of all— the sun.

Everyone gaped in stunned silence. Mr Hyde gave them a minute to take it in. Then he stood up, holding a plate of cakes.

'Greetings, Earthlings,' he cried. 'Observe

our wondrous solar system! I've even made my special moon rock cakes . . . '

Just then the classroom door burst open.

Barnaby! Jake froze. *Would he make a scene?* But he just sauntered to his desk and flung himself onto his chair.

'You nearly missed lift-off!' said Mr Hyde cheerfully. 'Now, where were we? Oh yes— well, of course the moon is not *actually* made of cake . . . '

RUSTLE RUSTLE.

Jake looked round. Barnaby was rummaging in his bag.

'Stop it,' Nora hissed.

Barnaby stopped. Jake glanced at him. He seemed to be listening intently to Mr Hyde. Maybe he was going to be okay, after all.

No—he saw a glint in Barnaby's eyes. What was he up to . . . ?

' . . . some believe it was created when a large asteroid hit Earth,' continued Mr Hyde.

Faster than a speeding asteroid, Barnaby whisked a paper plane out of his bag and launched it straight at Nora! Jake watched in horror as it sailed through the air, missed Nora, did a ninety-degree turn and crash-landed in the middle of Mr Hyde's moon rock cakes.

Jake held his breath. Mr Hyde would go mad!

But Mr Hyde picked up the plane, dusted the crumbs off and examined it.

'Nice plane, Barnaby,' he said, 'But not designed for a moon landing.'

Barnaby gaped at Mr Hyde in disbelief. *He thought that would make him angry*, Jake realized. But Mr Hyde just carried on.

'Which reminds me . . . on the 21st July 1969, the world held its breath as Neil Armstrong prepared to become the first human on the moon . . .'

With dramatic breath-holding and even a bit of moon walking, Mr Hyde acted out the story of the lunar landing. He made it seem almost real! Jake imagined the lunar module floating down, and felt as if he actually *was* Neil Armstrong, taking one small step . . .

All eyes were riveted on Mr Hyde as he picked up a remote control. He pointed it at the ceiling. With a shudder, the planets started to revolve, moving faster and faster.

'Oooooooooooh!' said the class, as one.

Mr Hyde walked among them, explaining,

'The planets move around the sun in a spectacular planetary dance . . .'

'YIPPEEEE-KI-AYEEEEEEEEEEEEE!'

Jake whirled round just in time to see a wild-eyed Barnaby jump on his desk and make one giant leap straight for Mars! He caught hold of it, and was whisked through the air straight for Jake. Jake ducked, and Barnaby's feet just missed his head.

'Yabba-dabba-doooo! Planet Barnaby coming throooough!!' he shouted gleefully, barrelling around the classroom. The solar system creaked horribly. Mr Hyde frantically stabbed at the remote control to stop it, but it sped up! Barnaby didn't look so happy to be joining in the planetary dance now.

'MAKE IT STOP!' he screamed, clinging on to

Mars for dear life. Pupils scrambled to get out of
the way of Barnaby's flying feet, but Alexis was
too slow and he thwacked her on the head.

'OW!' she cried. 'You idiot, Barnaby!'

She grabbed his leg and pulled as hard as
she could.

The solar system pulled the other way, as
hard as it could.

Something had to give . . .

Creeeeeeeeeaaaaaaaaaaak . . .

CRACK! Jake scrambled under his desk.

CRASH!

'Planet Barnaby' and the entire solar system crashed down onto the classroom floor.

There was a horrified silence. Jake lifted his head up.

Bits of planet lay strewn around the room. Mr Hyde stood shell-shocked in the middle of the chaos, Saturn's rings round his neck. As he slowly removed them, Jake saw his face turn almost as red as Mars. Soon, even his ears were crimson.

Jake stared. Mr Hyde was glowing. Just like the teacher had glowed outside the Head's office that morning. *So I didn't imagine it!* And what was that weird smell . . . sort of like burning rubber?

'Are you . . . are you okay, sir?' whispered Nora.

Mr Hyde didn't answer. He glowed even brighter, from the tips of his hair to his feet. Barnaby sniggered. The rest of the class sat in petrified silence. They had seen many teachers go red, some who had run screaming from the classroom, and one had been taken away in an ambulance. But none had ever lit up like a firework before!

By now, Mr Hyde was glowing so brightly that Jake couldn't bear to look at him. He closed his eyes . . .

BANG!

Then a popping sound. Like fireworks.

Wheeeeeeee . . . . like air escaping from a balloon.

And finally, what sounded suspiciously like a VERY loud fart.

RULE 5:

YOU MAY ^NEVER EAT PURPLE POWDER PAINT AND BOGIES

Jake slowly opened one eye, and then the other—and felt his jaw drop.

Where Mr Hyde had been standing, there was a cloud of purple smoke. Mr Hyde was nowhere to be seen.

There was a sudden whoop. Jake whirled round. It was Barnaby.

'Round One to me! I knew I could break him!'

'Shut up, Barnaby,' said Jake, shakily.

Barnaby grinned. 'That was epic!'

Jake glared at him. 'No, it was mean.' He stood up, took a deep breath and stepped cautiously towards the slowly dispersing cloud of smoke. 'He's gone!'

All eyes were on Jake. He realized they expected *him* to do something.

Great. He looked around. Where could Mr Hyde be? *He can't have vanished into thin air!* Then he heard a scuffling noise behind the teacher's desk.

'Mr Hyde?' Jake peered round the desk.

Nothing. Just a mouldy old banana skin.

Scuffle scuffle.

Jake leaned over and looked under the desk.

Nothing . . . No, wait . . . *What was that?*

In the corner, a fleck of light. He looked again. Eyes! Little glittering eyes . . .

Squatting under the desk was a small, hairy creature. And it was wearing Mr Hyde's glasses!

The creature stared inquisitively at Jake.

'Eeeee?' it squeaked.

Jake realized his mouth was hanging open. He shut it.

'Kipper-kipper-kipper-kipper-kipper!' chattered the creature.

Then it swung onto the desk and blew the longest, loudest raspberry Jake had ever heard. He thought it could even have made it into

The Guinness Book of Records.

It went on . . . and on . . .

Finally, it stopped.

Someone snorted. Someone else giggled.

Within moments, the whole class was roaring

with laughter. The creature giggled and blew several smaller raspberries as an encore.

Then it rocketed into the air like a mischievous missile.

SPLAAAAAAT!

It landed on Woodstock's desk.

'Arghhhh!' Woodstock yelped, and hid behind his fringe.

'Arrghhh?' The creature hid behind its fringe.

Woodstock couldn't help laughing. Then the creature saw a piece of paper sticking out of his bag.

'Eeeee?' It pulled the paper out. It was the drawing of Mr Hyde, still soggy with fruit juice. It nibbled a corner.

'Mmmmmm . . .'

'Hey!' Woodstock made a lunge for the

creature but it was too quick for him. It grabbed
his ruler and pole-vaulted off the desk. Alexis
and Karl dived under the desk as it flew towards
them, shrieking madly. It crash-landed on
Karl's desk, sending pens and pencils flying,
then skittered madly across desks to the back
of the classroom. Pupils scattered, giggling, as

it bounded towards them. This was the most exciting lesson they'd ever had!

The creature screeched to a halt in front of the School Rules poster. It stared at it with great interest. Jake had not read all the rules, but they included the following:

```
┌─────────── NOTICE ───────────┐
│                              │
│   DO NOT CLIMB ON THE DESKS. │
│       DO NOT LAUGH.          │
│     DO NOT PICK YOUR NOSE.   │
│ IF YOU HAVE ALREADY PICKED YOUR NOSE, │
│  DO NOT EVEN THINK ABOUT EATING IT.   │
│                              │
└──────────────────────────────┘
```

The photo of Mrs Blunt below looked even crosser than usual.

The creature climbed on the desk below the School Rules poster.

It laughed.

It picked its nose and ate the bogey (the creature didn't look as if it thought about it, admittedly).

Then it spotted a tin of purple powder paint sitting on the table below the poster. It stuck its head in the tin. Half a second later, its head came back out, looking purple and surprised.

'A-ə-ə-ə-əəəəəəəəəəəəəəəəəəəəəə CHooooooooo!'

Purple powder paint mixed with snot sprayed all over the School Rules poster.

Everyone gasped. Mrs Blunt was now wearing a large purple moustache, thick purple eyebrows, and purple hair. A huge bogey was stuck to her nose. Barnaby laughed so hard he fell off his chair.

Jake had to grin. Mrs Blunt somehow looked nicer with a purple moustache and eyebrows. He looked around for the creature, but it had vanished.

Karl, Alexis, Woodstock, and Nora ran over. They all started talking at once.

'Where's it gone?'

'What *is* it?'

'Where's Mr Hyde?'

'I think I know,' said Jake. They looked at him.

'It's wearing Mr Hyde's glasses. I—I think that creature IS Mr Hyde!'

Nora's eyes almost popped out.

'What—?'

From the ceiling came a squeak. The creature was hanging upside down on a light and stuffing purple paint into its mouth. It flung the empty tin away.

'BUUUUUURRRRRPPP!'

They stared up at the dripping purple furball.

'It's eaten a whole tin of paint,' said Nora, concerned. 'That can't be good for it.'

'If it is Mr Hyde, we have *got* to catch it before Mrs Blunt comes back,' Jake said. 'She'll definitely sack Mr Hyde if she finds out he's turned into a creature!'

'But how?' Karl asked.

'I'll climb up and rugby tackle it,' Alexis said, eagerly.

'No way,' said Nora. 'We should research what sort of creature it is. I'll get the Animal Kingdom book—'

'We've got to catch it first,' said Jake quickly. 'I'll do that. Alexis, stand guard outside the door and watch out for Mrs Blunt. Everyone else— tidy up!'

Barnaby walked over.

'I'll help you catch it,' he said, grinning.

Jake frowned. He didn't trust Barnaby. But at that moment, Alexis burst back into the classroom.

'MRS BLUNT'S COMING!'

The class sprang into a tidying frenzy. Jake started to climb on to the desk below the creature.

'No need for that,' said Barnaby.

Jake stared at him. 'Why not?'

Barnaby pushed Jake to one side and held an open sports bag underneath the creature.

It swayed, and moaned.

Then it barfed purple paint.

Mostly over Jake.

It let go of the light, and fell.

Right into Barnaby's bag. In a flash, Barnaby zipped it up.

Jake quickly wiped himself down.

'CLASS 5B. WHAT ON EARTH IS GOING ON?'

Mrs Blunt really was in a Very Bad Mood Indeed.

RULE 6:

ALWAYS ~~BE QUIET~~ ^BURP^ IN THE PRESENCE OF THE HEADTEACHER

'You have three seconds to return to your seats. One . . . two . . .'

Jake slid into his seat just in time. Mrs Blunt's piercing eyes swept the class. They fell on Nora.

'Nora Newton. Where is your teacher?'

'Um . . . he went to the storeroom, Miss.'

'I shall wait, then,' said the Headteacher, crossing her arms.

She suspects something, Jake thought. Mrs Blunt started to stalk round the classroom, scrutinizing the work on the walls.

Jake shot upright. *The School Rules poster!* Mrs Blunt would see the purple moustache and eyebrows. He raced to the back of the room, reaching the poster seconds before Mrs Blunt.

'What are you doing, boy?' she snapped.

'Errr . . . it's a lovely day isn't it?' blurted Jake.

Mrs Blunt glared at him. 'No, it is not. Now sit down before I give you a Sad Face.'

Nora ran over and stood next to him.

'Miss, do you want to see my slug collection?'

Mrs Blunt looked ready to implode. 'Back to your seats THIS INSTANT, unless you want to work on the Rockery after school!'

Nora threw Jake an agonized look. If they

moved, she would see the poster. If they didn't . . .

'BUUUUURRRRRRP!!!'

Jake gasped—the burp had come from Barnaby's bag. Mrs Blunt's eyebrows shot up.

'BARNABY MCCRUMB!' she roared.

Barnaby looked huffy. 'It wasn't m—' He stopped. Everyone glared at him. He shoved his bag under the table with his foot. 'It wasn't . . . my loudest burp, Miss!'

He opened his mouth and burped. A truly magnificent burp.

In three strides, Mrs Blunt was at the front of the classroom.

'Barnaby McCrumb. You've earned yourself an hour's work after school on the Rockery. Class 5b, when Mr Hyde returns, please inform him that I expect your performance tomorrow night to be the best in school. Otherwise . . . '

She frogmarched Barnaby out of the classroom.

Everyone started talking.

Karl thumped Jake on the back. 'I'd forgotten about the poster!'

'Never mind the poster—where's Barnaby's bag?' Jake asked anxiously.

Alexis ran to Barnaby's desk. 'Here!' She pulled it out. 'Do you really think that thing is Mr Hyde?'

An excited crowd gathered around Alexis. She unzipped the bag a tiny bit and peered inside. A furry arm shot out and grabbed her nose.

She zipped it up again hurriedly.

'You'll scare him! Give him to me.' Nora

'yowwwww!'

pushed her way through the crowd of classmates and grabbed the bag. 'There, there,' she soothed it. 'Now we need to find out what he eats . . . '

'Maybe slugs?' said Karl, slyly. Everyone roared.

'KARL!' Nora screeched.

If they start yelling, Mrs Blunt'll be back, thought Jake. He ran to Mr Hyde's desk and rapped loudly. Everyone looked at him.

'Shut up and listen, everyone! This is important. No grown-ups can know about Mr Hyde turning into a creature. And no one from any other class. This has to be our secret. Otherwise Mr Hyde will be sacked . . . '

' . . . and we'll get another Mr Sharp,' added Woodstock.

There was a chorus of groans.

Nora stood up. 'Everyone must swear an oath—'

At that moment, the bell rang for the end of school. There was a stampede for the door.

'Wait, you haven't sworn . . . ' Nora pleaded, but it was no good. Soon the only ones left were Jake, Nora, Woodstock, Karl, and Alexis.

'Now what?' asked Alexis.

Woodstock clapped his hands. 'Let's take him to your tree house, Nora!'

Jake's eyes widened. 'You've got a tree house?'

Nora nodded. 'Yes, but it's Top Secret, so you mustn't tell anyone. Only Woodstock, Karl, and Alexis know about it. And now you. Okay, we'll take him there.'

'I can't—I've got football practice,' said Alexis.

Karl jumped up. 'And I've got a guitar lesson. Sorry, got to go!' He ran off.

Jake picked up the bag with Creature in and headed out of the classroom with Nora and Woodstock. As they walked past the Rockery, they saw Barnaby struggling under the weight of a huge rock.

Jake stopped, feeling bad. 'Barnaby!' he called.

Barnaby threw his rock down, wiping sweat from his forehead.

'That was a great burp,' said Jake. 'Sorry you got in trouble for it.'

Barnaby shrugged. 'Whatever. Can I have my bag?'

Jake shook his head. 'The creature's still in there.'

'I'll take him home . . . ' Barnaby stretched out a hand.

Jake pulled it away. 'No, we're taking him to—' He remembered he wasn't supposed to mention the tree house.

'Aw, come on . . . It's my bag!'

'Sorry, Barnaby.'

'Hey, Jake!' Woodstock yelled.

Jake looked round. Nora and Woodstock were standing outside one of the windows to the main hall, waving at him. He ran over.

'What? What is it?'

Woodstock pointed to the window. 'In there . . . '

Jake peered in. His eyes nearly popped out.

Amelia was prancing around the stage wearing a black leotard, pink fluffy head

boppers, and pink sheets attached to her arms.
A ragged line of pupils trailed behind her, also in
costume. A tinny song piped over the speakers.

'Tra-la-la, tra-la-la!

Come one and all to the Butterfly Ball!

Jake realized that they were supposed to be insects. Amelia was presumably a butterfly. Her two friends were smug-looking bees. He also identified a sulky spider, a caterpillar made of four pupils under a sheet and several confused ants who kept tripping over each other.

'They're terrible!' whispered Nora, gleefully.

Jake nodded. But—hang on . . .

'Uh oh.' He pointed.

Just in front of the stage sat Mrs Blunt.

'Fabulous fluttering, Amelia!' she called. 'Ants—stay in line, please!'

The friends turned and started walking slowly out of the gate.

'That does it,' said Woodstock gloomily. 'Mrs Blunt will think they're brilliant, since she's helping them practise.'

'We've *got* to be the best at the Founders' Celebration,' said Nora. 'Or she'll get rid of Mr Hyde.'

They looked at the bag in silence.

'She'll definitely get rid of him if he's a creature,' said Jake. 'Come on, let's get him to the tree house. Then we'll have to try and get him to change back.'

RULE 7:

REMEMBER TO ~~UNDER~~ OVER
ALWAYS GO ~~UNDER~~ ^
THE FALLEN TREE

Here we are,' said Nora.

Jake nearly collapsed on the pavement in relief.
The bag was very heavy. He looked up at the
huge, rambling old house that Nora had stopped
outside.

'You live here?' he said, surprised. 'My house
is only up the road.'

'Cool! And I live round the corner,' said

Woodstock. 'We can walk to school together, if you like.' He started opening the gate. Nora stopped him.

'We'll go round the back. Dad's doing important work today,' she said, cryptically.

'Saving the planet?' asked Woodstock, grinning.

Nora gave him a look. 'Maybe.'

She led them up an overgrown alley, stopping at a green gate.

'Keep close to me,' she warned. 'Step where I step. Don't touch anything. Don't make sudden movements—'

Jake giggled. 'Can we breathe?'

'Yes, but quietly. I've got . . . security devices.'

'Booby traps,' Woodstock whispered.

Jake's eyes widened.

'Stick close to me and you'll be okay.' Nora smiled reassuringly at Jake as she pushed the gate open. Jake didn't feel reassured.

They stepped through the gateway.

Jake whistled. Monstrous plants towered over him, with flowers that looked like they could eat you alive! Nora set off through the dense undergrowth, shouting instructions. Jake tried to keep up, but was slowed by the bag. Soon she was completely out of sight.

Her voice floated back faintly.

' . . . around the puddle . . . under the fallen tree . . . '

'Wait!' Jake shouted. 'Under or over?'

No reply.

Woodstock crawled up behind him.

'Over,' he said.

Jake heaved the bag up and started to climb over the fallen tree.

'UNDER!' came a shout from over his head.

Jake threw himself backwards, landing on Woodstock. Woodstock yelped. The bag slid down and landed on Jake's head. Jake and the bag squawked. The boys picked themselves out of a pile of dead leaves, groaning.

Jake shook a woodlouse out of his ear and glared at Woodstock.

'Over?'

'Sorry,' said Woodstock, rubbing his head.

They crawled under the log.

'Up here!' Nora's voice floated down from the treetops. Jake looked up. Perched at the top of an enormous tree was a tree house. A rope ladder and assorted cables snaked up the trunk.

He slung the bag over his shoulder and started to climb.

Every muscle in Jake's body screamed as he climbed, and he could hear frightened squeaks coming from the wildly lurching bag. Gasping for breath, he reached the hatch. It flew open and Nora reached down, grabbing the bag from him.

'Thanks . . . ' Jake panted, hauling himself through.

He stood up, and gasped.

Test tubes full of lurid liquids lurked in one corner and something gruesomely green gurgled away in a glass beaker. A rickety bookcase leaned against the wall, stacked with hefty books with titles like *Learning to Love Gravity* and *Rocket Science for Beginners*.

Nora smiled proudly. 'Welcome to my laboratory!'

Woodstock's fringe flopped up through the hatch, followed by the rest of him. They stood looking at the whimpering bag.

'We should let him out,' Nora said. 'He's not happy.'

'Okay,' said Jake. He spoke to the bag.

'Mr Hyde . . . um . . . Creature? I'm going to let you out. Try to be good, okay?'

The bag twitched.

Nora leant over. 'And don't eat my experiments. They aren't good for the tummy.'

The bag grunted.

Jake held his breath, and unzipped the bag.

For a moment, nothing happened. Then . . .

'YIPPPEEEEEEEEEEEEEEE!'

Creature rocketed into the air. Jake fell over backwards. There was a rattling, and a shower of dust. Then silence. Jake peered around. Where'd he gone? Aha—there he was, crouching crossly on a beam in the roof.

'Okay,' Jake said, eyeing him nervously. 'We've got to turn Creature back into Mr Hyde before tomorrow night.'

'By the morning, really,' said Nora. 'So we can practise the poem.'

'Yeah—but how?' asked Woodstock, twiddling his fringe thoughtfully.

Nora took a medical encyclopaedia from the bookshelf and started flicking through it.

'What made him change in the first place?' Jake said.

'Maybe it's an allergic reaction,' said Nora,

pointing to a picture in the book.

Woodstock shook his head. 'An allergic reaction brings you out in a rash; it doesn't turn you into a crazy creature!'

There was a cackle from the ceiling. They looked up. Creature was gleefully swinging from the light bulb like a trapeze artist. He let go, flew through the air and landed on the bookcase, causing it to wobble dangerously. *Learning to Love Gravity* slid off, fell through the air and landed *WHUMP!* on Woodstock's head.

Woodstock yelped. 'OW!'

'You'll wreck my tree house!' Nora's cheeks were flushing with anger.

A light bulb went on in Jake's brain. 'Hey,' he said. 'You're going red.'

'Am I?' Nora put her hands to her cheeks.

'It's great,' Jake said excitedly. 'It's sort of what happened before Mr Hyde changed. Barnaby wrecked his Solar System. He got really angry . . .'

Nora clapped her hands. 'Of course! When he gets angry he changes into Creature!'

'Would making him happy change him back, then?' Woodstock wondered. He pulled out his sketchbook and started scribbling.

'What are you drawing?' Jake peered over.

Woodstock held up his picture: a grinning Creature lounging by a swimming pool, wearing sunglasses and slurping a huge ice cream.

'That's brilliant. Show it to him,' said Nora. 'It might make him change back.'

'Creature! I've drawn your portrait!' Woodstock called. No answer. Creature had disappeared again. 'Where's he gone?'

Nora gave a shriek.

Creature was squatting among the paraphernalia on Nora's desk. He was clutching two test tubes—one full of green goo, one fizzing with orange stuff.

'My stink bomb!' Nora cried in horror.

Jake and his friends prepared to dive on the giggling Creature.

'HEE-EE-LLLLPPPPPPPPP!'

Jake and Woodstock froze. A scream had come from below the tree house. Milliseconds later, a red light by the door started flashing and a siren wailed. Creature dropped the test tubes and shot behind the bookcase, gibbering in fright.

'What's happening?' shouted Jake, hands over his ears.

Nora walked calmly to the door and switched off the siren. She smiled grimly.

'*Someone's* got caught in my trap!'

RULE 8

TELL ~~NO~~ EVERY ONE, ABOUT
THE TOP SECRET
TREE HOUSE

The two boys raced to the window, but it was hard to see anything through the leaves. Jake turned to see Nora fiddling with an ancient TV set.

'It's hooked up to a camera,' Nora explained. 'It'll show us who's in the trap.'

A fuzzy image began to appear on the screen. Jake held his breath. *Who could it be?*

As the picture flickered into focus, Jake saw a bedraggled figure yelling and thrashing about in a net hanging about a metre off the ground.

'Barnaby!' they all exclaimed together.

'What's he doing sneaking about in my garden?' Nora said, angrily.

They looked at the screen. Barnaby's arms and legs were poking out of the net, like a fly caught in a huge web. Woodstock giggled. Jake and Nora started laughing too.

'Not yabba-dabba-doo-ing now, is he?' Woodstock grinned. 'Shall we leave him there?'

'Tempting, but I'll have to let him out,' said Nora. 'You two go down while I lower the net and keep an eye on Creature.'

Jake and Woodstock clambered down the ladder to the struggling Barnaby. As they reached the bottom, Jake heard a loud CLUNK from the tree house. The net and Barnaby crashed heavily to the ground in an explosion of dirt and leaves.

Barnaby crawled out of the net and stood up, dripping with mud and covered in leaves from head to foot. He shook his head, dislodging a family of woodlice from his hair. Jake and Woodstock had to laugh.

'Yeah, yeah, very funny!' Barnaby fumed. 'I've

just had to lug about two million stupid rocks from one side of the school to the other and now you guys are trying to kill me!'

'Sorry,' said Jake, trying to keep a straight face. 'But you did look funny.'

'What are you doing in Nora's garden, anyway?' asked Woodstock.

'I wanted to help you with the creature,' said Barnaby, sulkily.

'But how did you know to come here?'

Barnaby laughed. 'Easy. Nora's always going on about her not-so-secret *Top Secret* tree house! I knew you'd bring him here.'

Jake sighed. 'Well, now you're here I suppose you might as well come up.'

They helped Barnaby out of the net and climbed back up the ladder. Barnaby went first.

When he got to the hatch, Nora was there to greet him with an icy glare.

'Say the password,' she snapped.

'I don't know the password.'

'Well then, you can't come in.' She crossed her arms.

'Nora, let him in,' Jake called up. 'He's soaked through. And he'll say sorry for sneaking around. *Won't you*, Barnaby?'

'Oh—yeah. Sorry.'

'Well . . . ' Nora relented. 'Okay. For five minutes. But don't touch anything. And you'll have to swear an oath—'

But Barnaby had already scrambled up into the tree house. His eyes lit up.

'Wooooh . . . awesome den!'

'It's not a den, it's a laboratory,' said Nora,

pernickety as ever.

He walked over to the desk with all the test tubes on it.

'These are well cool! What's in here?' He picked up a flask and shook it.

'That's my homework!' Nora grabbed it off him.

Barnaby put his hands up. 'Okay, keep your wig on! So where's the creature, then?'

Jake had almost forgotten about Creature in all the kerfuffle. He ran to look behind the bookcase. Creature's eyes glittered in the shadows, but when he saw Jake he hissed and his hair stood on end. He scrambled up the shelves and squatted on the top, twittering.

'Come down, Creature,' said Jake. Creature didn't move.

'He was scared by the siren,' said Woodstock. 'Has anyone got any food we could give him?'

Jake and Nora shook their heads.

'I have,' said Barnaby. He fished around in his pocket and brought out a custard cream.

'Is that all you ever eat?' laughed Woodstock.

Barnaby looked affronted. 'I sometimes have Hobnobs.'

Jake took the custard cream from Barnaby and waved it in the air.

'Here, Creature, a nice bicky—OW!'

Creature had hurled a book down at him.

Nora took the biscuit. 'Creature, you really should eat something, you know,' she called, holding the biscuit up. She jumped back as another book was launched into the air.

'Silly thing! Can't you see we're trying to help

you?' she cried.

'Let me try.' Barnaby took the biscuit back from Nora. He walked over to the bookcase. He didn't say anything, just held the biscuit out on the flat of his hand.

Creature stopped twittering. He swung himself down until he was sitting on a shelf opposite Barnaby. Barnaby still didn't speak, just held the biscuit out. Creature made a crooning noise, then reached out a furry paw and took the biscuit. He nibbled it contentedly. Barnaby withdrew his hand and looked smugly at the others, who were all staring at him, flabbergasted.

'How come you're so good with him?' asked Nora.

Barnaby shrugged. 'I've got five dogs at home. I'm good with animals.'

'Five dogs?' Jake was incredulous.

'My mum's mad about dogs,' said Barnaby.
'She says they're nicer than people.'

Creature finished the biscuit and jumped on
to Barnaby's shoulder.

'Can I take him home?' asked Barnaby,

eagerly. 'I promise I'll look after him.'

Jake shook his head. 'He's staying here tonight.'

Barnaby looked disappointed. Nora looked at Jake.

'I don't think it's a good idea to leave him here,' she said, slowly. 'He'll cause chaos, and he might escape. I think you should take him home, Jake.'

'Me?' Jake gulped. 'Why not Barnaby? He wants to. And he's good with Creature.'

'He's got five dogs. They might scare him.'

'I'd take him, but my gran seriously would have a heart attack if she saw him,' said Woodstock.

Jake sighed. *It was up to him, then.*

'Fine, I'll take him,' he said. 'Barnaby, you'd better show me what you did with that biscuit . . . .'

RULE 9:

~~DO~~ NOT LEAVE YOUR
LITTLE SISTER IN CHARGE
OF A CREATURE

I'm late! The corridors were eerily empty as
Jake hurtled towards the final corner before
the classroom. Where was everyone? And what
was that clicking noise? He skidded round the
corner . . .

CLICK! CLICK!

He screeched to a halt. A stag beetle as big
as a rhinoceros stood in front of the classroom

door. Oddly, it had dark hair and a painted-on, purple moustache.

Mrs Blunt! She's turned into a giant stag beetle!

'JAKE JONES! Did you paint this moustache on me?' She lurched towards Jake, clicking her huge pincers threateningly. Jake tried to run but his legs turned to jelly . . .

He woke with a start.

Just a dream!

Maybe the whole thing with Creature was a dream, then? *But—what's that on top of me?* He tried to sit up, but couldn't. He peered over the covers.

'Kipper-kipper-kipper-kipper-kipper!'

Groan. *Not a dream.* Creature was crouching on his chest, wearing Jake's Spiderman pants on his head. When he saw Jake, he squeaked. Then he bounced off towards the door.

Somehow, Jake got there first.

'No you don't!' he exclaimed, slamming it shut. It burst open again.

'LOST MY TEDDY!'

Connie! His sister was only three but she was already nearly as big a pain as Amelia.

'Teddy—not—here,' he grunted, trying to hold the door closed, but she bulldozed her way in, and spotted Creature.

'FUNNY DOGGY! CONNIE KISS DOGGY!' She waddled towards Creature, arms outstretched.

'Yik!' Creature pulled a face. Connie flung herself on him affectionately and yanked out a handful of fur. He squawked and ran into a corner. Connie shrieked in fury.

'DOGGY NO RUN 'WAY!'

She made a flying leap for Creature, grabbing his nose and nearly knocking his glasses off. That was the final straw. He hurled himself sideways, ran up the curtain and perched on the curtain rail, trembling.

Jake had an idea.

'Connie—STAY HERE. I'll put *Best Dressed Pets* on, okay? Just don't leave the room . . .'

He grabbed some clothes from his wardrobe and managed to pull them on at the same time as sprinting to the TV and putting Connie's favourite programme on. *She won't move now,* he thought, *and nor will Creature while she's in the room.* Then he ran to get breakfast. He sloshed milk over a bowl of Fruitloops and was about to dash back upstairs—

'Hello, Jake.' Mum was blocking the doorway.

'Hi Mum. I've just got to—'

'Why did you go straight up to your room yesterday?' His mum looked concerned. 'Didn't you like your first day at school?'

No, Mum, it's fine,' Jake insisted. 'I like it.'

'Well, Granny was disappointed not to see

you,' his mother went on.

'Oh, sorry. I forgot Granny was staying over,' Jake mumbled.

'Actually, she was supposed to be coming next week but she got her dates mixed up and—'

BRIIIIIIIIIIIIIIIIIING! The phone rang.

'For heaven's sake . . . ' Mum went to answer it. Out of the corner of his eye, Jake spotted a small furry lightning bolt shoot past the kitchen door. Two seconds later, Connie waddled past at top speed, crying.

'SILLY DOGGY! WON'T PUT NAPPY ON!'

Jake nearly dropped his Fruitloops.

'Yes Alan, the paperwork's ready . . . ' Mum was saying. Jake edged out of the kitchen and ran down the hall. *Where'd Creature go?* He heard a voice from the living room.

'Is that you, Jakey? Where's my kiss?'

Granny!

He screeched to a halt outside the door.

'Have you grown a beard, dear? Goodness, children grow up fast nowadays!'

Puzzled, Jake pushed the door open.

Creature was squatting on Granny's lap, puckering up his lips . . .

'NOOOOOOO!!!' yelled Jake. Creature shot straight upwards in fright and landed on the lampshade. Luckily Granny was quite deaf.

'You don't want a kiss then?' she asked.

'What's all this yelling?'

Jake whirled round. Dad walked in with a cup of tea. 'It's a madhouse here today. First Connie and now you. Here's your tea, Mum—'

FAAARRRRRRTTTTTT!

An explosive fart noise erupted from the lampshade! Jake gulped. Dad would be sure to see Creature now! But he just put the tea down and frowned at Granny.

'Mum! Have you been eating baked beans? You know they don't agree with you.'

Granny blinked. 'Who doesn't agree with me?'

Dad shouted. 'BAKED BEANS!'

'BAKE BEAN! BAKE BEAN!' Connie was in the doorway, laughing hysterically. Jake looked up for Creature. He'd vanished.

'David, did you open the front door?' he heard Mum call.

'No!' Dad shouted back. 'More importantly, where are my car keys? They're not where I left them!'

Jake had a terrible thought. *Creature!* He shot to the window and pulled back the curtain.

Yup—there he was, trying to start the car! Jake pelted outside, past his startled dad, just in time to grab the keys. Creature chattered angrily and dived onto the back seat. Dad appeared in

the doorway. Jake held the keys out to him.

'Here are your keys, Dad . . . they were in the car . . .'

'Were they, indeed?' Dad looked suspicious, but looked at his watch. 'I've got to get going.'

He got in the car and revved the engine. Jake panicked: Creature was in the car—the car was rolling down the drive . . .

'DAD!' Jake ran after it. Dad wound the window down.

'Can you give me a lift to school? I'm going to be late . . . '

Dad rolled his eyes. 'Be quick.'

Phew. Jake ran indoors, grabbed Barnaby's bag, and ran out again. He jumped in the back. Creature was curled up asleep on the floor.

'Let's have the news,' Dad said, switching the radio on. With some difficulty, Jake managed to stuff the sleeping Creature into the bag.

' . . . *on a lighter note, pupils at a local school are celebrating its fiftieth anniversary today with a special Founders' Celebration. The Headteacher spoke to our reporter this morning . . . '*

'That's your school, Jake,' said his dad. 'Fame at last!'

Jake laughed weakly and did a quick sum.

Six hours to go! And still no sign of Creature changing back . . .

Dad pulled up at the school gates just as the caretaker was just closing them.

'Watch it!' the caretaker exclaimed as Jake swerved through, clutching the bag. He ran at breakneck speed across the empty playground, burst through the door . . .

SMACK!

. . . and crashed straight into Barnaby McCrumb.

RULE 10:

BOYS AND CREATURES ARE ~~NOT~~ PERMITTED IN THE GIRLS' TOILETS

Hi Jake,' said Barnaby, grinning. 'I'll have my bag back now, thanks.'

Jake gripped it. 'No, Barnaby,' he said crossly. 'Creature's asleep. You'll wake him up.'

Barnaby grabbed the bag. 'I want to see him!'

With a yank, Barnaby wrestled the bag from Jake, but the weight took him by surprise and it fell to the floor with a thump.

'SQUAAAARK!'

The bag started lurching around violently.

'Now look what you've done,' exclaimed Jake.

STOMP. STOMP. STOMP.

He froze. Footsteps were coming down the corridor. Jake and Barnaby looked at each other in panic. They had to hide Creature—but where?

'In here.' Barnaby grabbed the bag and ran to the nearest door.

'That's the girl's loo!'

'We don't have a choice . . . ' Barnaby ran in. Jake followed him, heart hammering.

STOMP. STOMP.

Silence.

'Who's in there? You should be in class!' A familiar voice said loudly from right outside. 'I'm the prefect and I'm going to tell.'

'It's Amelia,' hissed Barnaby. 'Quick, get in a cubicle!'

They squeezed into the end cubicle and Barnaby put the bag on the toilet seat. Thankfully, Creature had gone quiet.

Creeeeeeeeeeeeeeaaak.

That was the door. Jake held his breath.

'You're in trouble now, whoever you are.' Amelia's voice echoed around the toilet.

Her footsteps came closer.

BANG!

Both boys jumped. They crouched down and peered under the door. Jake could see Amelia's feet walking along the row of cubicles. She was banging each cubicle door open.

BANG! She was only two doors away.

There was a sudden noise above him. Jake glanced up, just in time to see Creature shoot out of the bag! He swung gleefully on the toilet chain, lost his grip and tumbled into the next cubicle, with a surprised squawk.

Jake froze. Within seconds, Amelia would open that door and see Creature!

'I know you're in there,' Jake heard her

hiss. He had to do something fast! He pushed Barnaby to one side and threw the cubicle door open. Too late.

BANG!

Creature shrieked.

'KIPPER-KIPPER-KIPPER-KIPPER-KIPPER!'

Jake saw Amelia's face drain of colour.

'BUUUUUUURRRRRRRRRRRRRRRRP!'

Creature belched right in the trembling girl's face.

Amelia screamed 'MUMMMMMMY!'

Then she collapsed in a heap on the floor.

'What's happening?' hissed Barnaby from inside the cubicle.

'Amelia saw Creature and fainted,' said Jake, running over to her. Barnaby came out.

'Great. She'll go straight to Mrs Blunt,' he said, looking down at her.

'We can't let her do that,' said Jake. He thought frantically. 'When she wakes up, we'll say it must have been a dream or something—'

Amelia groaned. Creature was still bouncing around, squeaking.

'We have to get her out of here!' hissed Jake.

The two boys dragged Amelia out of the toilet and into the corridor, propping her up against the wall.

'I'll stay with her—you go back in and get Creature in the bag again,' said Jake.

Barnaby disappeared into the toilet.

Amelia groaned again.

'Amelia!' Jake said in her ear. No response.

'WAKEY WAKEY!' he said louder, shaking her shoulders. Her head shot up and her eyes popped open. She stared at Jake.

'The new boy!' she exclaimed. 'What are you doing? Why am I here?'

'I heard a crash in the toilet so I went to see what was happening,' said Jake. 'You must have fainted. You were dreaming, muttering something about a creature.'

She stared at him. Then her face went pale.

'That wasn't a dream—there really was a monster! A nasty smelly little monster . . .

it shouted "kipper-kipper-kipper" and burped at me . . . with horrid little eyes, and . . . and—it was wearing GLASSES!'

'Monsters aren't real, Amelia,' Jake said, patting her hand. 'You've just had some sort of dream or—or a hallucination or something.'

Amelia pushed his hand away impatiently.

'I'll show you, if you don't believe me!' she cried.

At that moment, Barnaby walked out of the toilet with the bag over his shoulder. *Great timing, Barnaby*, Jake thought. *I should have warned him to stay put.*

Amelia's mouth dropped open.

'Barnaby McCrumb! What're you doing in the girls' toilet?'

Barnaby shrugged. 'I thought it was the

boys'.' He started to walk away.

'WAIT!' shouted Amelia. Barnaby stopped.

'There's . . . something . . . in the toilet.' Her voice faltered.

Barnaby grinned. 'Yeah. Sorry. It wouldn't flush.'

Amelia stared at him in horror. 'Ugh—I didn't mean that! I mean a monster!'

'Yes, it was, wasn't it,' said Barnaby, grinning even more.

Amelia went bright red. She turned to Jake.

'New boy! Tell him what I saw.'

'She saw a monster wearing glasses that said "kipper" and burped at her,' said Jake.

Barnaby laughed. 'Oh yeah—I saw it too.' He deepened his voice. 'Its Burp Power was strong, but mine was stronger, and I finally cast it down into the Bog of Beastliness for all Eternity.'

Amelia glared at him. 'You think you're so funny—'

Barnaby's bag suddenly squawked.

'KIPPER!'

Amelia's eyes nearly popped out.

'Did you hear that? That was it! *The monster!*'

The two boys looked at each other and shook their heads.

'I didn't hear anything,' said Jake.

'Me neither,' said Barnaby.

'You're still hallucinating,' said Jake.

'Kipper–kipper–KIPPPPERRRR!'

Amelia started quivering and pointed at the bag.

'It's in there—in your bag! It said "kipper-

kipper-kipper"! You *must* have heard that!'

Barnaby looked at the bag. 'Nah—it's just my sports kit. It doesn't talk.'

Jake had a sudden brainwave. He put on a concerned expression.

'Amelia, do you think you might need to go home, or see a doctor or something?'

Amelia went pale. 'Why?'

'Well, you're clearly not very well, if you're imagining monsters. You probably shouldn't even do the Founders' Celebration tonight. It might just—tip you over the edge . . . '

Amelia went paler. 'I have to do it, I'm the Star of the Show!'

Barnaby got the idea. He shook his head sadly. 'Mrs Blunt would definitely say not to— '

'*What* would I definitely say not to do?'

Mrs Blunt was standing not three metres away, with a face like thunder.

RULE 11:

PLAYING OF POPULAR
MUSIC IN SCHOOL IS
~~STRICTLY~~ REQUIRED ~~FORBIDDEN~~
Λ

Jake and Barnaby shuffled awkwardly. Amelia staggered to her feet.

'Mrs B-Blunt,' she stammered.

'Amelia? Are you all right?'

'I'm fine, Miss!' squeaked Amelia. 'I'm really . . . excited about to the Founders' Celebration tonight!'

Mrs Blunt looked closely at Amelia.

Then Barnaby. Then Jake.

'If you don't tell me what's happening,' she said coldly, 'you boys will both be working on the Rockery all day.'

Jake felt his heart thumping painfully. One false move and he could give the whole game away. He had to say something, though.

'Well, Miss . . . Amelia says she saw something . . . '

Amelia yelped. 'I didn't see anything, Miss, I'm really fine!'

She's desperate to perform at the Founders' Celebration, thought Jake.

Mrs Blunt fixed Jake with a stare. 'What did Amelia see?'

Out of the corner of his eye, Jake saw Barnaby suddenly shift nervously and shove the bag behind him with his foot. Mrs Blunt saw.

'What's in that bag?'

Barnaby gulped. 'It's . . . it's just my sports kit, Miss!'

'It just moved! Let me see.'

She darted round Barnaby and grabbed one of the handles. Barnaby yelped.

'Miss, I really wouldn't! It's—a bit stinky! It hasn't been washed for a year!'

Jake chimed in. 'It's disgusting. It's actually growing things . . . '

Barnaby nodded. 'I'm giving it to Nora to do some experiments on. She thinks there are life forms in there that exist nowhere else on the planet.'

Mrs Blunt dropped the bag handle as if it had burned her. Then she looked at the white-faced

Amelia, and shook her head.

'Poor child,' she said. 'Come with me.'

She started walking her down the corridor.

'No one should have to witness Barnaby McCrumb's dirty sports kit.'

As Jake and Barnaby walked into the classroom, the buzz of voices died away. Karl was strumming a guitar, but he stopped when he saw them. All eyes turned to Barnaby and the bag.

Nora's face fell. 'Is he still Creature?'

Jake nodded glumly. A disappointed murmur ran around the room.

'Better let him out, Barnaby,' Jake said. Barnaby unzipped the bag.

For a moment nothing happened, then Creature's dishevelled head appeared. He squawked, shot out of the bag and headed

straight for the fish tank, where he stuck his head under the water and started blowing raspberries at the fish.

'Oh, leave them alone, Creature,' Nora said. But she didn't move.

Creature pulled his head out and shook it, spraying water everywhere. Then he bounded across desks and jumped on to Mr Hyde's chair. He grabbed a pen, cackled, and started scrawling 'CREATURE WOZ ERE' all over the whiteboard.

The class sat in gloomy silence. No one had the heart to try and stop him.

Nora sighed. 'And don't forget—we've got to rehearse the Joy of School Rules for tonight.'

Woodstock groaned.

'The Joy of School Rules! That's a joke. School Rules Blues more like . . . '

Karl strummed a chord.

'I got the School Rules Blues,' he sang, softly. 'I'm in trouble again . . . '

As Karl started playing, Jake happened to glance at Creature. Something very strange happened.

Creature stopped scrawling on the board and began swaying to the music, a dreamy look on his face. As soon as the music stopped, the

dreamy look vanished and he started scrawling and cackling again.

That's it!

'Karl!' shouted Jake. 'Play that again!'

Karl looked questioningly at Jake.

'It did something to Creature!'

Karl started strumming again.

'I got the School Rules Blues, I'm in trouble again . . .'

Creature stopped scrawling and looked at Karl. Then he looked at Jake and squeaked.

He wants me to join in!

Jake clicked his fingers. Creature made a soft clicking sound, and looked at the rest of the class. It dawned on Jake. *Not just me—everyone!*

'Everyone—join in!' he called.

The class looked hesitantly at each other.

Jake felt desperate. He knew this was going to work—*had* to work! But how to get everyone working together—

'Wa-ah-wa-ah-womp-womp!
Chuppa-chuppa-chomp-chomp!
Doo-wup doo-wup a diddy-dum-diddy-doo!'

Drums? Jake spun round.

The drum noises were coming from Barnaby's mouth! Jake watched, amazed. It sounded just like real drums and cymbals!

Barnaby's a human beatbox!

Karl played faster, in time with Barnaby's beatboxing. It was impossible not to tap your feet, and before Jake knew it, everyone was clapping in time!

'I got the School Rules Bluuuues, I'm in trouble agaaaain . . . ' sang Karl.

Alexis ran to join him.

'I got a Creature for a teacher . . . ' she sang.

Woodstock looked up. 'And it's driving me insane . . . '

'I'm just trying to do my lessons . . . ' sang Nora, adjusting her glasses.

'He's trying to climb up the drain!' Jake finished the verse, grinning.

Karl and Barnaby carried on playing, and one by one, everyone joined in, singing a line each, and grabbing things to beat out the rhythm—pens, pencils, rulers—whatever was to hand. Jake got so into it that he almost forgot Creature—but not quite.

He looked back to the front of the class.

Creature had hopped onto the teacher's desk and was crooning softly, completely wrapped up in the music. His eyes glowed behind his glasses, getting brighter and brighter. His whole body started to light up with a pulsating orange glow and every hair on his body stood on end. The music faltered as the class gawped in astonishment . . .

'Keep going!' Jake shouted.

Everyone sang together. 'We got the School Rules Blues . . . '

Creature was now a blazing ball of brightness so intense it was painful to look at him. A pile of papers where he was resting smouldered and burst in flames . . .

'I'm in trouble again . . . '

'KIPPERRR-RRR-RR!'

The glowing ball of Creature let out a deafening war cry and swung himself under the teacher's desk.

The room went dark.

'... Creature ... for a ... teacher ...' the voices wavered. The music died away. A loud thrumming noise was coming from under the desk.

Nora covered her ears. Jake covered his eyes.

Barnaby covered his lunchbox.

FAAAAAAAAAAAAAARRRRRT!

Wheeeeeeee.............

POP! POP! POP!

BANG!

RULE 12:

DON'T YOU REMEMBER
RULE 11? I SAID ~~NO PLAYING~~
PLAY THAT FUNKY MUSIC
~~OF POPULAR MUSIC!~~
∧

Twenty-six pairs of eyes were riveted on the teacher's desk.

For a moment, nothing happened. Then the desk shuddered. There was a groan . . .

'MR HYDE!' cried Nora, jumping to her feet.

It worked! Jake breathed a sigh of relief and beat out the flames that had ignited the papers.

It was, indeed, Mr Hyde. He stood up. His

hair was wild and his glasses were crooked, but apart from that he looked exactly as he had looked before he changed into Creature.

There was a cheer.

'Are you all right, sir?' cried Nora, running up to him.

Mr Hyde gazed around as if unsure of where he was. He straightened his glasses and focused on Nora.

'Oh dear,' he said. 'Please tell me what I think just happened *didn't* happen?'

Nora looked uncertain. 'I think it did, sir.'

Mr Hyde sat down heavily on his chair.

'What did I do?' he asked in a dismal voice.

There was a pause.

'Um . . . You ate paint,' said Woodstock.

'You gave Mrs Blunt a purple moustache,' called Karl.

'You tried to kiss my granny,' added Jake.

Mr Hyde winced.

'Okay—I've heard enough,' he said despondently. 'I owe you an explanation.'

The pupils leaned forward expectantly.

'A few years ago, I started having strange dreams,' Mr Hyde began. 'At first I didn't take any notice—they were just dreams, right? In these dreams, I would turn into a creature. Sometimes large, sometimes small. Always badly-behaved.'

'You were some sort of monkey,' said Alexis.

'Crossed with a Tasmanian Devil,' added Nora.

He nodded. 'That's what it usually is. After a while I noticed that when I woke up my back door was open and the neighbours' gardens had been turned upside down. Then I realized—the dreams I'd been having *weren't* dreams. They were actually happening!'

'Weren't you scared?' whispered Nora, eyes wide.

Mr Hyde nodded. 'Of course. I locked all my doors and windows at night to stop myself getting out. But it got worse. I started changing in the day.'

'What makes you change?' asked Jake. 'Is it when you get angry?'

'Angry, sad, happy—any strong emotion can set it off. I never know how long it'll last, or what I'm going to do—' he looked at the class, suddenly anxious. 'You won't say anything to anyone, will you? They'd send in scientists, hook me up to things . . . '

'NO!' everyone exclaimed.

'We won't, sir. We already agreed that,' said Jake. Mr Hyde looked relieved.

'Well, I'm glad I changed back before I did anything really awful,' he said. 'Jake, I wish I could apologize to your granny . . . '

Karl had been bursting to speak.

'Sir . . . music changed you back. We wrote an awesome song for you.'

Mr Hyde looked at him. 'Really?' he said. 'I'd love to hear it—' He stopped, and smiled sadly.

'But I don't think you'll be wanting a creature for a teacher. I'm sorry, 5b, but I'm going to hand in my resignation.'

He stood up and walked towards the door.

Every pupil in the class jumped up.

'NO!'

Jake shot to the door and blocked his way.

'You can't leave,' he said, firmly. 'You're a brilliant teacher!'

'The best,' added Woodstock.

'Your dancing was . . . inspiring,' said Karl.

'Your solar system was amazing!' said Nora.

'Your moon rock cakes were scrummy,' said Barnaby, grinning.

Mr Hyde blinked. 'Do you—do you really mean that?'

'YES!' everyone shouted.

Mr Hyde scratched his head. 'Well . . . I could give it another go.'

'HURRAY!!' Everyone cheered. Mr Hyde flushed and grinned happily.

'You really are the best class in the world! I'd better do some teaching then, hadn't I! What's on the menu for today's learning extravaganza?'

Nora and Jake exchanged looks.

'We have to practise for the Founders'

Celebration tonight,' said Jake, grimacing.

Mr Hyde clapped his hands. 'Of course! The Joy of School Rules! Okay, everyone in position! Hop to it, folks!' Mr Hyde bounded around, moving tables. He stopped, and looked around. 'What's the problem?'

There was silence.

Woodstock plucked up courage. 'Sir, no one wants to do the poem.'

Karl nodded. 'It's s-o-o-ooo boring.'

'No one can remember the words,' said Alexis.

'Plus it's factually inaccurate,' added Nora.

Mr Hyde scratched his head. 'I see your point. But we have to do something . . .'

Karl put his hand up. 'We could do our song!'

Mr Hyde's eyes twinkled. 'The song that made me change back? Excellent idea! Let's

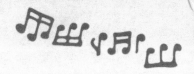

have a listen then.'

'Yessss!' Karl grabbed his guitar and marched to the front. 'Ready, Barnaby? Everyone? **THE SCHOOL RULES BLUES!'**

Jake and his friends began to sing just like they did before. Then the whole class joined in the chorus:

'We got the School Rules Blues,
But that's not going to bring us down!
We've got a creature for a teacher,
He's small and furry and brown . . .
There ain't no teacher like him—
He's the best teacher in town!'

The last chord rang out.

Mr Hyde sat stock still. Everyone shuffled nervously.

Then he leapt up, clapping furiously.

'HOLY KIPPER! That was amazing! Karl, I take my hat off—and Barnaby, extraordinary! All of you—you rock!'

'Can we do it at the Founders' Celebration, then, sir?' asked Nora.

Mr Hyde laughed. 'Of course! It'll go down a storm! We'll have to change some of the words, of course . . .'

Flushed and excited, everyone started talking. But something was bothering Jake. He beckoned to Barnaby.

'What about Amelia?' he whispered. 'What if she changes her mind and says something about

Creature in the girls' toilet?'

Barnaby winked. 'Leave Amelia to me.'

RULE 13:

ALWAYS
~~DO NOT~~ SNORE IN
SCHOOL
PERFORMANCES

'Drive faster, Dad!' urged Jake. They were horribly late because Connie had hidden the car keys in the toilet.

'We're stuck in a traffic jam, Jake,' said Dad.

Jake's mum pointed. 'The pavements are jammed too. They must all be going to the Founders' Celebration!'

Jake looked out. It was true—everyone was

heading for the school. His stomach lurched at the thought of being on stage in front of all those people. As the car inched closer to the gates, he spotted Nora just outside them.

'Stop the car, Dad. I'll get out here . . . ' Jake jumped out.

'Break a leg!' his dad called, as he drove off.

Nora rolled her eyes as he ran over to her. 'Where've you been? Mr Hyde told me to come and find you!'

'When *are* we on?' asked Jake as they headed through the gates.

'Second—after 5a. We've got about twenty minutes.'

Diving between swarms of twitchy parents, they raced through the gates and down the corridor to the changing room. As they burst through the changing room doors, a deafening wall of noise hit Jake's ears.

'Who's on first?'

'I've lost my wings!'

'Where are those pesky ants?!'

Nora beckoned to Jake. 'This way.'

Mr Hyde was giving Class 5b a pep talk as they approached.

'Remember—you are winners! Repeat after me: WE ARE WINNERS!'

Class 5b mumbled: 'We are winners . . . '

'Again! WE—Ah, Jake and Nora,' said Mr Hyde. 'Are we all here now? Where's Barnaby?'

Jake looked around. Barnaby was nowhere to be seen.

Nora frowned. 'He was here earlier.'

'We can't do it without him!' exclaimed Karl.

The loudspeaker in the corner crackled.

'FIVE MINUTE CALL FOR CLASS 5A. 5A, TAKE YOUR POSITIONS BACKSTAGE!'

Mr Hyde stood up. 'We'd better go too—we're on after 5a. Don't worry, Barnaby will turn up.'

They trooped out of the changing room to the backstage area. It was jam-packed with fidgeting, whispering pupils. Jake looked around for Barnaby, with no luck. He bit his lip. Karl was right—the song wouldn't work without Barnaby and his beatboxing. *Where could he be?*

Suddenly, he heard a sharp, bossy voice over the hushed whispers.

'Not like that, Kaylee! Pin it *higher*—no, higher, I said! And Sonia, you didn't fix my antennae on properly, they keep slipping off!'

Amelia, thought Jake, wincing. He looked

around. Yup, there she was, flouncing about in her humungous, horrid pink and yellow butterfly costume. Her two friends, in bee costumes, were fussing round her while she yelled orders at them.

'Where's my water?' she screeched. 'Someone bring me water!' A harassed ladybird scuttled off for water.

'I know what I'd do with that water,' he heard a whisper in his ear. 'Pour it over her head.' It was Woodstock. Jake grinned at him.

'Yeah, me too.'

'Let's go and wait in the wings,' said Woodstock. 'You can see the audience from there.'

They wormed through the mass of pupils to the side of the stage, pulled the curtain back a tiny bit, and peered out. Jake scanned the crowd for his parents and spotted them near the back. *Mum looks nervous.* He gulped. *We have to get this right!*

The buzz of voices died away as Mrs Blunt climbed the steps and clicked across the front of the stage in the highest heels Jake had ever seen.

There was a soft 'pop' as she turned the microphone on.

'Welcome, everyone. This evening, we are delighted to welcome our esteemed Founders–'

'ZZZZZZZZZZZZ-Z-Z-Z-Z-Z-Z . . . '

A loud snore interrupted Mrs Blunt's speech. She stopped, flustered.

Jake peered round the curtain and saw four incredibly old people sitting in the front row. Two men and two women, silver-haired and as wrinkled and grumpy as rhinoceroses.

'The esteemed Founders,' whispered Woodstock. Jake tried not to giggle.

One of the Founders was fast asleep, with his mouth wide open. It was from here that the snore had erupted.

'Wake up, Harold!' hissed the woman next to him, whacking him over the head with her handbag. He woke up and looked blearily around.

'What's that, dear?' he quavered. 'Supper's ready, you say?' and then went straight back to sleep.

Mrs Blunt continued between gritted teeth.

' . . . *to welcome our esteemed Founders, who established this school fifty years ago on such excellent rules . . .*'

'ƧƧƧƧƧƧƧƧƧƧƧƧ-Ƨ-Ƨ-Ƨ-Ƨ-Ƨ-Ƨ . . .'

Jake thought, by the look on Mrs Blunt's face, she was probably at this very moment devising

Rule 143: 'No Snoring in School Performances'. Grinning, he turned to share this thought with Woodstock, but Woodstock suddenly clutched Jake's shoulder and gasped.

'What—?' Jake began, but then he stopped and stared across the stage.

Barnaby was loitering in the wings on the other side of the stage. He was talking to Amelia, who was smirking and handing a bag to Barnaby.

Jake gasped too. 'She's giving him sweets!'

'Quick—we've got to stop her!' said Woodstock, fiercely.

Jake and Woodstock started fighting their way across the sea of Class 5a insects, who were all pushing and shoving to get ready to go on.

'Barnaby!' called Jake across the sea of heads, but Barnaby didn't hear. Amelia held the bag out . . . Barnaby reached out his hand . . .

'We're too late,' panted Woodstock. They finally reached Barnaby. He saw them, and winked. Then he pushed the bag of sweets away.

Puzzled, Amelia stared at the bag, then at Barnaby.

'Go on—they're your faves.' She held the bag out again.

Barnaby shook his head and grinned at her.

'Seen any monsters recently, Amelia?'

'Wha-what?'

'KIPPER-KIPPER-KIPPER!' Barnaby hissed.

Amelia froze. The colour drained from her face, and the bag dropped from her hand. It landed on the floor with a thud and burst, sending hundreds of little round sweets rolling everywhere.

Barnaby grinned. Then he opened his mouth.

'Buuuuuuurrrrrppp!'

'YOU? *You're* the m-m-monster?' stammered Amelia.

RULE 14:

WHEN THINGS GO WRONG, ~~REMAIN~~ CALM

PANIC!

Amelia backed away from Barnaby towards the stage, a look of terror on her face.

' . . . *to start us off, Class 5a, performing* The Butterfly Ball . . . ' Mrs Blunt was saying.

Barnaby took a step towards Amelia.

He burped again.

' . . . *starring the exceptionally talented* AMELIA TROTTER-HOGG!' declared Mrs Blunt.

With a shriek, Amelia backed right
onto the stage, in full view of the
audience. As she did so, her feet
hit some of the rolling sweets and
shot out from under her. Jake watched,
open-mouthed, as the exceptionally
talented Amelia Trotter-
Hogg flew across

the stage in a not-very-butterfly-like way—and skidded smack into Mrs Blunt!

Mrs Blunt tottered, swayed, then fell off the the stage . . .

WHUMP!

. . . landing on top of the snoring Harold, whose mouth was still wide open. As she did so, his false teeth shot out and attached themselves to Mrs Blunt's nose. Jake, Barnaby and Woodstock, peering round the curtain, nearly died laughing.

'HELP! I'm being attacked!' squawked Harold. Harold's wife, who had also fallen asleep during Mrs Blunt's speech, woke up.

'Get off my husband!' she shrieked, and began bashing the red-faced Mrs Blunt over the head with her handbag.

'Ow! Sorry! Ow!' squeaked Mrs Blunt, fending off blows. She managed to disentangle herself from Harold and crawl away from the frenzied handbag attack, Harold's false teeth still firmly attached to her nose. She ripped them off, looked around wildly, and then shouted at the pianist.

'Music, Mavis!'

The startled pianist launched into a song. Amelia staggered to her feet, flapping her wings weakly. As the two bees buzzed onstage, the pianist realized she was playing the wrong music and stopped. The confused bees tried to retreat, but got caught in a spider-web prop, where they hung, thrashing and squealing.

Finally, the pianist found the right music but started playing at double speed. Amelia tried to keep up, but flapped so fast one of her wings fell off. The front end of the caterpillar had an argument with the back end, and broke in half. Meanwhile, the ants milled around getting in everyone's way.

Jake could not believe his eyes. It was chaos. And out of all the pupils on stage, Amelia was the worst. *Even Connie could do better*, he thought.

The Founders clearly weren't impressed, either.

'What *is* this?' asked one.

'Some modern twaddle,' said another.

'It wouldn't have happened in my day,' snapped Harold's wife, waving her handbag menacingly in Mrs Blunt's direction.

Finally, The Butterfly Ball fizzled out. There were a few nervous claps as Class 5a shuffled dejectedly off stage. Jake, Woodstock and Barnaby looked at each other.

'We're on now,' whispered Woodstock, looking pale.

'Remember, folks—WE ARE WINNERS!'

Jake looked round. Mr Hyde and the rest of Class 5b were right behind him.

On stage, a flustered Mrs Blunt took the

microphone.

'*Thank you, 5a—a very, errm . . . interesting performance . . . anyway, who's next? Oh yes, Class 5b, reciting a poem written by me.*'

She beckoned frantically to Mr Hyde.

' . . . afraid they've not had much time to practise . . . ' she was saying as Mr Hyde led the class onstage. Jake looked out into a sea of expectant faces. He swallowed, his mouth suddenly dry. *This is it.*

Mr Hyde took the microphone.

'You're right, Mrs Blunt, they haven't had much time,' he said, 'But they're a very talented bunch of kids, and I know they'll give a performance to remember. Ready, everyone?'

Karl stood up, guitar at the ready.

'One, two, *one-two-three-four!*'

He launched into the song. Jake felt his foot
start tapping.

'We got the School Rules Blues . . .
Every boy and every girl . . . ,'

There were hoots and whistles from the audience as Barnaby started to beatbox. A few people started clapping to the rhythm.

'We got a brand new teacher . . . He's really out of this world . . . ,'

As Jake sang his line he caught a glimpse of his mum and dad grinning and waving madly at the back. A stream of crazy rhythms flew out of Barnaby's mouth, Nora and Alexis danced madly, and Karl played a fantastic guitar break. By the last verse, the whole audience was clapping, whistling, and dancing. Even the Founders were tapping their feet!

Mrs Blunt wasn't clapping, whistling, or dancing. She had her arms crossed, a look of white fury on her face. As the last chord rang out, she stalked onstage.

'I'm sorry . . . this was not my poem—'

'BRAVO!'

Jake blinked. *Who was that?*

Harold! The elderly Founder was on his feet, clapping like mad. Mrs Blunt paused, confused.

'There's been a mistake—' she began.

'ENCORE!' Harold's wife was standing too, waving her handbag.

Mrs Blunt's mouth opened and closed like a fish out of water.

'BRAVO! ENCORE!'

Everyone was on their feet, shouting for more! Jake and his classmates looked at each other, flushed and excited.

We did it, Jake thought proudly.

'ENCORE!' the crowd roared.

Mrs Blunt looked as if she might collapse.

'Well ... maybe ... just this once ...' she said faintly.

Mr Hyde smiled and turned to the audience.

'Ladies and gentlemen—let's hear it again for the Fabulous 5b Band!' He strode to the piano. 'I'll join you on piano ... take it away, Karl!'

In a daze, they started to play, with the audience singing along. Mr Hyde was an incredible pianist, and captivated the crowd instantly. The spotlight swivelled to focus on him. He played faster and faster, till his hands were a blur . . .

Jake stared. Something wasn't quite right.

Was smoke coming off the keys? It smelt like . . . burning rubber! That spotlight was way too bright! Jake shielded his eyes . . .

Oh no!

It wasn't the spotlight—Mr Hyde was glowing! He glowed brighter and brighter . . . till even the tips of his hair crackled . . .

Beside Jake, Nora gasped. He jumped up.

'Quick!' he shouted. 'The curtains!'

Jake and Nora sprinted to the curtains and

pulled them across, just as Mr Hyde disappeared in an explosion of white light!

Jake took the microphone.

He bowed. 'That's all folks! Thank you, and good—'

'BUUUUUUURRRRRPPP!'

SCHOOL REPORTS

JAKE JONES

JAKE JONES
REPORT SUMMARY

Jake is a sociable, intelligent boy. He is fitting into his new class well, has already made some very good friends and is clearly a natural born leader. He's an action person with the ability to think fast and act on his feet. He's willing to take risks and stand up for himself and others, often taking the initiative in difficult situations. I feel Jake has a great future as a firefighter or policeman. Maybe even the Prime Minister! He needs to practise his funky dance moves however—very important for a Prime Minister, of course.

SIGNED: *Mr E. Hyde*

BARNABY McCRUMB

BARNABY McCRUMB REPORT SUMMARY

Barnaby is a lively character, whose main interest seems to be chaos theory at which he excels. He is also skilled at paper aeroplane design and propulsion. His gardening skills are improving no end, as he has had a lot of practice on the Rockery. His main talent, however, is burping, and while I'm not sure exactly what practical use this will be in his future career, I have no doubt he will go far—preferably as far as possible.

SIGNED: Mr E. Hyde

NORA NEWTON REPORT SUMMARY

Nora is a highly intelligent girl with an impressive knowledge of science and the natural world. Her specialism is slugs, and has on several occasions had to be told to remove them from her classmates' packed lunches.
Although I like to encourage pupils' interests, it is hard to do that when they are grey, slimy and crawling around in your pasta salad. Nora can sometimes be a bit bossy—sorry, assertive—but it is nice to see that she seems to be spending more time with her friends and less time with creepy crawlies now.

SIGNED: Mr E. Hyde

NORA NEWTON

WOODSTOCK STONE

WOODSTOCK STONE
REPORT SUMMARY

Woodstock is a very creative individual who's never happier than when he's dabbling around with a paintbrush or pencil. His portraits are excellent, although I fear the one he did of the Headteacher is not accurate—she doesn't actually have flames coming out of her nose. He is a very positive and relaxed pupil, for whom everything is either 'cool' or 'awesome'. Although the school is happy for pupils to express their individuality, I do feel Woodstock is in need of a haircut, as his fringe keeps dipping in the paints.

SIGNED: Mr E. Hyde

KARL McQUEEN
REPORT SUMMARY

Karl is an outgoing boy who is happier on stage than off it. He is very gifted at music, which he applies to all subjects. He is ambitious and often talks about his intention to appear on the 'Totally Talented Teens' TV show. He does need to apply himself more in other subjects—for example, while his musical interpretation of the nine times table was interesting, it wasn't actually correct. However, since his chosen career is to be a member of a boy band, mathematical accuracy will probably not be an issue.

SIGNED: Mr E. Hyde

KARL McQUEEN

ALEXIS WILLIAMS

ALEXIS WILLIAMS
REPORT SUMMARY

Alexis is a sporty pupil whose main aim in life is to get the ball in the back of the net. Her first love is football, although she also likes rugby, basketball, tennis— pretty much any sport actually. Getting her off the pitch and into the classroom can be difficult and she does need to realise that sports kit is not actually school uniform. Alexis is fearless both on and off the pitch and has been known to tackle players twice her size. However, as the school nurse has asked me to point out, she does need to remember that not every problem in life can be solved with a flying tackle.

SIGNED: Mr E. Hyde

CREATURE
REPORT SUMMARY

Creature is an energetic character who shows enthusiasm for many curriculum areas. He is very 'hands on' in his approach to problem-solving—for example, in answering the question

CREATURE

'Is purple paint edible?' he simply ate it, with unfortunate and lurid results. He needs to build his awareness of health and safety. His main talents are swinging manically from the ceiling and making realistic fart noises, which I suppose could lead to a glittering career in childrens' TV. But I always feel there is another side to Creature and if only he would just let it out he would be a much more rounded individual.

SIGNED: Mr E. Hyde

MR HYDE

MR HYDE
REPORT SUMMARY

Mr Hyde is totally the Best Teacher in the World! He is much better than Miss Read or Mr Sharp because he actually doesn't make us clean the toilets with toothbrushes. He likes Dancing and Yoga but isn't very good at them. He made the Solar System in the classroom and it went round and lit up and everything. And it fell down but that wasn't his fault. He is totally fantastic on the Piano. And he wears cool glasses. But the totally weird thing about him is . . . oops, sorry I nearly forgot—actually that's Top Secret!

SIGNED: Nora Newton   Jake Jones

AMELIA TROTTER-HOGG
REPORT SUMMARY

Amelia is one of our Outstanding Pupils, excellent in every way. She makes everything she touches sparkle with fairy dust and happy music seems to play whenever she skips gracefully into view. She is a very talented singer and dancer and shows all the makings of a 'prima donna'. Amelia is always willing to help the Headteacher when it comes to discipline and is therefore a wonderful role model for other pupils. Her brilliance inspires devout loyalty in her small but select group of friends, who never leave her side. Excellent work, Amelia!

AMELIA TROTTER-HOGG

SIGNED: Mrs Blunt

POP!

SOMETHING'S OUT OF CONTROL IN THE CLASSROOM... AND FOR ONCE IT ISN'T THE KIDS

CREATURE TEACHER GOES WILD

SAM WATKINS and ILLUSTRATED BY David O'Connell

Creature Teacher Goes Wild

Jake's class is going to the opening of Wilf's Wild Adventure Theme Park. The theme park has some amazing rides, but things get a bit too wild when Mr Hyde ends up turning into Creature and causing chaos on the Ghost Train! Will Jake and his friends be able to track down Creature and get him to turn back into Mr Hyde before the truth about their teacher gets out? It's going to be a rollercoaster of an adventure!

About the author

Sam Watkins voraciously consumed books from a young age, due to a food shortage in the village where she grew up. This diet, although not recommended by doctors, has given her a lifelong passion for books. She has been a bookseller, editor and publisher, and writes and illustrates her own children's books. At one point, things all got a bit too bookish so she decided to be an art teacher for a while, but books won the day in the end.

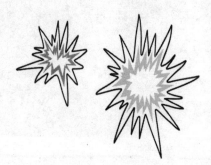

About the illustrator

David O'Connell is an illustrator who lives in London. His favourite things to draw are monsters, naughty children (another type of monster), batty old ladies, and evil cats . . . Oh, and teachers that transform into naughty little creatures!

Here are some other stories that we think you'll love.